Wrong Time, Wrong Place
By Dave Weston

Chapter one

"Mum! Dad! Quick, come and look at this!"
"What? What is it?" asked [...] down the stairs. She was use[d ...] usually for some non-event like [...] it was different. Nick grab[bed ...] outside instead of into the li[ving room? ...]et and what she saw shocked her. [...] here quick. Call an ambulance! Nick, [hone]y, I don't want you to see this, come inside."
"No way Mum! Besides I've already seen it so what's the point of trying to hide it from me now? I hope she's OK. I saw it all happen."
"You saw? Tell me what happened." Before Nick could tell his mum anything, his father interrupted him, "Ambulance is on its way. I heard a bang when I was upstairs. What the hell's happened?" As he looked up the street, he could make out the shape of a body lying underneath the canopy of a tree and a car with half of its front embedded in the tree. Its bonnet was up and there was smoke pouring from the radiator, a faint hissing noise was slowly subsiding.

Nick Knight was a typical 11 year old who tended to get a bit too excited over the smallest of things. Some saw this as enthusiasm, others thought it was annoying but Nick did not care what people thought of him. The day of the accident, Nick was playing basketball on his drive. He was supposed to be playing with his friend, Martin, but he had to stay in because he had not done his homework, which was of no surprise to Nick. Martin was always getting into trouble for not doing his homework, what surprised Nick was that Martin's mum had bothered to check. Nick was a bit disappointed as he had been looking forward to playing football with Martin but he was forced to play basketball because his mum hated him banging the ball against their garage door.

He had been practicing his lay-ups and slam-dunks and he had sensed a real improvement so he decided to practice his long range shooting, the three-pointers. Sadly, he had been less successful with these and was starting to get tired running up and down collecting the basketball. It was then he heard the booming noise. Nick looked up to see where the noise was coming from. At first, he could not see anything but then a beautiful Mercedes SLK turned into his street. The booming noise got louder and Nick realised the Mercedes had a loud sound system in it, as it passed him he could even hear some of the lyrics. It sounded like Eminem although he was not sure but he did know it was rap music.

As the car approached him, he could see the driver was a woman who was nodding her head in time to the beat of the music. He was glad she was driving slowly because he really liked the shape of the Mercedes. He had been into cars ever since his Dad had taken him to a motor show. Sports cars were his favourite, he liked the way they looked and the noise they made when you revved the engine. He had also noticed that people stop and stare when they see a sports car and so he thought that everybody liked them. This car was silver with big, shiny wheels. Nick had seen SLK's before and they never had those wheels on so he guessed that the woman had bought them herself. The woman must have seen him looking because she started to go faster and Nick listened to the roar of the engine as she accelerated.

As the Mercedes sped past his house and neared the end of his street, Nick heard a loud crack and suddenly the car swerved violently to the right. He stood there with his mouth open as he watched the Mercedes go up the pavement and the whole of the back of the car seemed to glow red as the driver slammed on the brakes. It was too late. With a sickening bang, the car smashed into the tree. At almost the same time, he heard the sound of glass breaking and then, to his horror, he saw the woman fly out of the windscreen and onto the ground, underneath the tree. "Oh no!" whispered Nick to himself.

For what seemed like minutes, Nick stood there looking at the car, then the body, then the tree and back to the car. He tried his best not to look at the body again. Everything had gone silent. One minute he could hear booming from the stereo, the engine revving and tyres screeching, the next all he could hear was the hissing from the radiator.

There was movement, Nick looked around and saw people starting to come out of their houses. He had not moved. He still had his basketball in his hand. As he looked up the street, opposite to the crash, Nick saw something unusual. There was a man in a black, hooded top, standing looking at the car. The man started to look around and he spotted Nick looking at him. Nick got a good look at his face but it was not for long because the man covered his face, tucked something under his top and ran backwards down the alleyway in which he was standing. Nick thought this was strange because everyone else was walking slowly towards the wreckage but this man seemed to be in a hurry to get away from it. "Mum! Dad! Quick, come and look at this!" he shouted.

Chapter two

Nick had never been so excited although he thought his parents did not seem to share his excitement. Here he was, in a real police station, surrounded by real coppers and they were about to interrogate him! "Wait until Martin hears about this!" Nick exclaimed, "He's gonna be so jealous! I'm gonna tell him they tried to beat me up because I wouldn't tell them anything!"

"You will not!" whispered his dad as he knelt down beside him. "The police are not here to interrogate you, they are here to question you about what you saw so you make sure you tell them everything and do not lie to them."

"Why would I lie to them?" asked Nick.

"I don't know, you know what you're like, Nick. You get so excited, you get confused about what actually happened and what you thought happened."

"No I don't! Thanks a lot, Dad. I'm nervous now."

"Don't listen to him sweetheart," said his Mum, "you just go in there and tell them exactly what you saw, OK?"

"That's what I told him to do!" protested his Dad, but he soon shut up when Mum gave him one of her looks.

"OK, Nick? I'm Detective Saunders and this is Detective Sealey. Would you like to come with us? We need to ask you some questions." Both of the detectives looked huge to Nick. Detective Saunders was a big man with shaven hair. Nick thought he was old because his skin was wrinkled and he had big bags under his eyes. Detective Sealey was a tall woman with long brown hair. She was younger than Saunders and Nick could not help but notice her bright pink lipstick. "Martin would fancy her!" he thought to himself, stifling a giggle.

Nick and his parents were taken into a room that had Interview Room 4 on the door. Nick was disappointed because it did not say

Interrogation Room. "Right then, Nick. This is how this works," explained Detective Sealey in a friendly voice, "we're going to ask you some questions about the accident, OK?"

"OK." replied Nick. He sat down and had a look around the room. He was not as excited now. The room was quite dark and he started to feel a bit nervous.

"Now, just in case we forget something you tell us," continued Sealey, "we're going to tape our chat so that we can listen to it another time and not have to drag you back in here. Is that alright?"

"Yes." Nick answered. He liked Detective Sealey and he started to relax a bit. Detective Saunders just sat there looking at him and whenever he looked at the policeman, Saunders gave him one of those fake smiles that all adults do when they don't know what to say to you. Sealey pressed the record button on the tape recorder.

"Right then. Now, you saw the accident in your street this afternoon, didn't you, Nick?" asked Sealey.

"Yep, I did." said Nick.

"Can you tell us exactly what you saw, Nick? Take your time and try not to leave anything out." Nick slowly started to explain what happened. He started from the beginning and definitely never left anything out. He even told them about Martin always forgetting to do his homework and about the motor show his dad took him to. Nick noticed that when he was talking about the motor show, Sealey smiled but Saunders just rolled his eyes and looked at his watch.

Eventually, Nick finished his account. "Thank you, Nick," said Detective Sealey, "now, you said you heard a loud crack just before the car crashed. What do you think that was? Did you see anything?"

"No, I think it was the tyre bursting. Am I right?" asked Nick; during the interview he decided he wanted to be a detective.

"You could be. Right, we don't need to ask you anything else," said Sealey as she turned off the tape recorder, "thanks for all your help,

Nick, you're a very observant boy. You would make a good policeman."

Nick smiled, stood up and stretched, that comment made him feel very proud of himself. "Really? Thanks!" He was just about to open the door when he remembered something. "Oh, I forgot to tell you about the man." Saunders turned the tape recorder back on and gestured for Nick to sit down again. "What man?" he asked, it was the first time Saunders had spoken. Nick started to explain about the man in the black top and how he ran away when he saw Nick looking at him. "Did you see the man? Can you describe him to us?" asked Saunders.

"Err, I think so. He ran away when he saw me looking at him. Yeah, he put something under his top and ran away." Nick yawned, he had not realised how tired he was until they started asking him questions again. "Can't we do this again in the morning?" asked Nick's mum, "My son is getting very tired, he's had a very long day." Saunders and Sealey looked at each other, Saunders nodded. "OK, Mrs Knight," he said, "but before you go, can we have a word with you and your husband alone? Nick, can you wait outside for us please?" Nick did not like this one bit, he told them everything he knew and now they were going to keep something from him. He reluctantly stood up, "Go on son, just wait outside. We won't be long and we'll stop for a McDonalds on the way home." said Nick's dad. This made Nick move quicker and he stepped outside into the corridor and watched the door shut behind him.

Nick looked out of a window for a while and then remembered how annoyed he was that his parents were being told something that he wanted to know. He went back to the door and put his ear against it. He could not really hear anything, every sound was muffled but he recognised Detective Saunders' voice was doing most of the talking. Nick heard footsteps coming towards the door and started to step backwards when he heard his mum's voice saying "Oh my God!" Nick wondered what she had been told and he started to worry. The door opened and Nick looked at his mum, she was smiling but it was one of those fake smiles that adults do when they don't know what to say to you.

Chapter three

After such an eventful weekend, Nick was glad to go back to school and tell all his friends about what had happened. Of course, Martin was really jealous that Nick had been interrogated and wished that he had done his homework earlier so that they would have both witnessed the accident. Nick knew that he had not really been interrogated but thought that Martin did not need to know too. He felt good to be back at school among his friends, people of his own age and not a lot of strange adults like he was at the weekend. However, once he got home, his whole mood changed because his parents had been weird ever since they had left the police station.

When Nick went to bed on Monday night, he lay awake trying to think about what the detectives had told his parents and whether his parents had given anything away without realising it. He really wanted to be a detective now and he saw this as his first case. The drive to McDonalds was fairly quiet, Nick had asked what the detectives had said but his mum and dad just changed the subject and told him how proud they were of him for being so good. His mum had been particularly strange that evening, Nick had heard her crying and his dad saying that everything would be OK. Even stranger was the fact that she came and tucked him in to bed that night and told him she loved him when normally he goes to bed himself. Despite all this, Nick could not think of what his parents had been told but he had a sneaking suspicion that the man in the black top had something to do with it.

Towards the end of the week, Nick was sitting next to Martin in another boring Music lesson. His class had just finished listening to some ceremonial music from Indonesia, or some other exotic place that Nick did not care about, when he looked out of the window. Nick scanned the view, he could see the tall office buildings of the city in the background and the tops of hundreds of houses as his eyes came to the foreground. He was so bored that he decided to count the rooftops. After he had lost count, his eyes looked across the school's walls and what he saw there stopped his daydreaming instantly. There, sitting on the school wall, staring at him was the man in the black top. He was still wearing a black hooded top but was also wearing a baseball cap, baggy jeans and trainers. Nick made a note of all this because he remembered Detective Sealey's words about having to be observant to be a good copper. For about one minute, Nick and the man just stared at each other. A thousand thoughts raced through Nick's mind: what was he doing here? How did he know I was here? Is he looking for me?

Nick was interrupted by Martin who nudged him and whispered, "What are you looking at? You'd better be careful or Mr Sneddon will catch you daydreaming."
"Mart, it's him. He's outside." Nick replied.
"Who? Santa Claus?" Martin giggled at his own joke.
"No stupid, the man from the accident. The one who saw me looking at him and ran away."
"Everyone runs away when they see you for the first time, mate!" Martin had to try really hard not to laugh out loud, he was on a roll.
"Get lost! He's there and he's just staring at me. Look." Nick hissed. Martin was starting to get on his nerves; he had been trying all week to play the accident down so that Nick did not get all the attention from their friends. Martin checked that Mr Sneddon was not looking his way and leaned across Nick to see out of the window. Sure enough, the mysterious man was still sitting there on the wall. "See him?" asked Nick.
"Yeah. Hang on, what's he doing? He's putting his hand in his pocket……oh, he's just lighting a cigarette."
"BOYS! What on earth are you doing? What is so fascinating out there? Is it more fascinating than the gamelan music of Indonesia?" Mr Sneddon had caught them and he was not happy. "No, sir," replied Martin, "it would have to be mighty fascinating to be as fascinating as gamelan music, sir." Nick put his head in his hands, Martin could never resist being sarcastic even if it got him into

trouble. "Well, you'll be able to find out more about it in the detention I'm giving you for being so rude, won't you, Martin?"
"Yes, sir." groaned Martin who made a mental note to think before he opens his mouth in the future.
"Knight, what were you two looking at out there?" Mr Sneddon had turned his attention to Nick.
"There's a man sitting on the wall, staring at me, sir." Nick explained, he did not want a detention, his parents would kill him. Mr Sneddon walked over to the boys' table and looked out of the window. Nick looked out at the same time and was stunned to see that the man was no longer there. "I can't see any man, Knight!"
"He was there, sir, I promise. He was sat on the wall just staring at me!"
"Hmmm, a likely story, now pay attention or you'll be joining your friend in detention!" As Mr Sneddon walked back to the front of the class, Nick had a final look out of the window. He could not see the man now but there, at the corner of the school wall, a puff of cigarette smoke drifted up into the air.

Chapter four

Nick could not stop thinking about what had just happened at school, he hardly spoke to Martin on the way home and his mum noticed he was quieter than usual when he got home. "What's the matter, honey?" she enquired.
"What? Oh, nothing, I'm fine. Just tired."
"Everything OK at school, Nick?"
"Yeah, why shouldn't it be?" Nick had been thinking about the incident in music for a long time and was starting to think that the man staring at him had something to do with what the two detectives had told his parents. He was not sure about his theory but what else could it be? Why else would the man come back? He was being kept in the dark about something and he was not happy about it.

Nick spent the rest of the night trying to figure out a way of getting his parents to tell him what the detectives had said. In the end, he decided to tell the truth and bring some of his acting skills into play. "Mum, Dad, can I talk to you please?" he asked in his most innocent voice.
"What is it son?" asked his Dad.
"At school today I saw the man from the accident sitting on our wall and he was just staring at me. It was weird and a bit scary. Why do you think he was there?" Nick noticed his mum had put her hand to her mouth. "Did he do anything, Nick?" his Dad's voice sounded serious, Nick realised that after seeing his parents' reaction, he was no longer acting scared, he was scared. "No, nothing, he just sat there looking at me and had a cigarette. I told Mr Sneddon about it but when he came to look out of the window, the man had disappeared." Nick's mum had gone pale, she didn't say a word, she just looked at her husband who looked back at her. "Right, I'm calling Detective Saunders." Nick's dad got out of his chair and walked to the phone.

"Detective Saunders? Why?" asked Nick, inside he was congratulating himself; not only had he guessed right about the police having something to do with all this but it also looked as if he was going to find out what the detectives had told his parents.
"Mum, what's going on?" he asked in that innocent voice that had taken him months to perfect. "We'll explain in a minute, Nick, let's just hear what Detective Saunders has to say."
"Saunders said he'll come round right away," said dad as he got off the phone. He looked at Nick, "I suppose you're wondering what this is all about?"
"Yeah, I am a bit," replied Nick.
"You'd better sit down then," said Dad.

Chapter five

"You see, Nick, the police think that the man you saw had something to do with the accident."
"Why?" Nick enquired, even though he had suspected it himself.
"Well," continued his Dad, "when the police looked at the car they found a bullet in one of the tyres…"
"So it was a gun shot that made the car crash? That must have been the crack sound I heard!" Nick thought aloud. His dad smiled to himself, "You know, Nick, you're too perceptive for your own good sometimes – you would make a good policeman." Nick smiled at the compliment but became serious again when he realised what he was being told, that and the look on his mum's face.
"You see honey, the woman driving that car was the girlfriend of a nasty person who lives in the city and the police think she was killed to send a message to that person."
"I don't understand." Nick frowned.
"You see, it's like this," began his dad, "there are two rival gangs in the city. You may have heard about them – the Boss Street Crew and the Panthers. Basically they steal, sell drugs and vandalise places and try to control what they see as their territory. They have always hated each other but up until now it has always boiled down to arguments and sometimes, fights."
Nick remembered something he saw in the local newspaper a few weeks ago. "I read about this in the paper," he said, "it said they were fighting more and more."
"That's right," explained his dad, "you see they both want to control the same part of the city and whoever controls it gets to sell drugs in it which means they make more money."
"Why don't the police do something about it?" asked Nick.
"They are trying Nick but it is difficult because the gang members stick up for each other. If the police try to arrest one of them, the other gang members say that they were with them whenever they were supposed to be committing a crime." his mum explained.

"Anyway, the other week, the Boss Street Crew attacked and beat up the best friend of the leader of the Panthers. He's still in hospital now, the papers are saying he might die." his dad continued. Nick could not believe what he was hearing. He knew bits about the two gangs but because he lived just outside the city it all seemed miles away from him and something he didn't need to worry about. He was excited about everything that had happened at the weekend but now he was scared. What he heard next made him go from feeling scared to feeling terrified. "The police think that the accident, well murder, I suppose," said his dad, "was a revenge attack by the Panthers on the leader of the Boss Street Crew. Basically they are saying to him, "If you beat up our friends, we will kill the ones you love." The police were concerned when they heard you say that the man in the hooded top saw you looking at him, now that he's been at your school, they are worried that he might try and get you because you saw what he did."

Chapter six

"Bill! Don't say that! You're scaring him to death!" shouted Nick's mum. It was true. Nick felt the colour drain from his face as his brain processed the words coming from his dad's mouth: a man who has already killed one person could be after him. To Nick everything went quiet, even though he could see his parents' mouths moving, he heard nothing. All he could think about was the man's face staring at him from the school wall. Then something awful dawned on him. Sound began to filter back into Nick's mind. "I think it's for the best Sue," his dad was saying, "Nick is old enough to understand the situation. He has the right to know what's going on." Nick's mum was about to reply to that but Nick beat her to it. "Oh God!" he shouted. He felt sick with worry. "This man who might be after me, he knows where I live and he knows which school I go to!" Nick jumped up and was walking around the room. His legs knew he should be moving but his brain didn't know where to go. Nick's parents stood up and hugged him. "Listen, son," said Nick's dad soothingly, "we have told Detective Saunders about him being at your school. He and Detective Sealey are on their way now and they are going to move us somewhere safe. Do you understand me?"

The fact that his dad was staying calm helped Nick become calmer too. He took a few deep breaths and let everything he had just heard sink in. Somehow, he didn't feel too scared anymore. He realised that he would be safe if the police were moving him and his family somewhere else. He looked at his dad and then across to his mum who was weeping. "Come on, Mum," he said, "you shouldn't be crying. After all, it's me they're after!" Nick's mum laughed through her tears and stroked her son's face but the tears didn't stop until Detectives Saunders and Sealey arrived.

Chapter seven

"Hello Nick, it's nice to see you again," smiled Detective Sealey as she sat down with the cup of coffee his mum had made her. Detective Saunders stood by the fireplace and did one of his grins again. Nick wondered if Saunders had children of his own, and if he did, if he ever spoke to them. "Now then, your mum and dad say you had an unwanted visitor at your school today. Can you tell me about it?" asked Sealey. Once again, Nick was exhausted after explaining everything to the two policemen but was aware that he felt a lot calmer than he did before they had arrived. "This Mr Sneddon sounds a bit of a strict teacher" mumbled Saunders. Nick smiled, he was shocked that Saunders had tried to make a joke but was glad that he did, it made him feel safer. If Saunders wasn't worried, why should he be? "He is," replied Nick, "could you arrest him for me?" This time it was Saunders' turn to smile.

Detective Sealey suggested to Nick's mum that she might like to start packing a few essential things because they were moving to the safe house that night. As Nick's mum busied herself with that task, Sealey spoke to Nick and his dad. "Now, Nick. Your dad tells me he's told you everything he knows. I don't want to scare you but your mum and dad agree you should know everything that is going on." Nick smiled gratefully to his dad. He would prefer to know the situation rather than be kept in the dark. Sealey pulled a photograph from her pocket. "From the description you gave us at the police station, we believe this is the man you saw on the day of the accident and the man who came to your school today." Nick looked at the picture carefully. He saw a young man, probably in his mid-twenties with brown eyes and scruffy black hair. The man looked tough as if he didn't care he was being photographed by the police. Nick had never seen his hair before because the man was wearing a hood when he saw him but from the shape of his head and the glare in his eyes, it was clear that this was the man who was now after him.

Nick nodded, "Yeah, that's him." he stated. Sealey nodded with him. "OK. This is Leon Fairbanks. He is a known member of the gang called the Panthers. He has a criminal record for offences such as burglary, drug dealing, assault and, from what you've told us, it looks as though we can add murder to that list as well. He has been in jail for assault before but was released late last year."
"I was the one who arrested him," explained Saunders, "he's a nasty piece of work. No respect for authority, he spat at me when I arrested him. He loves the Panthers, to him they're his family and he would do anything for them, although I never expected things to go as far as this." This didn't make Nick feel any better. Sensing his anxiety, Sealey smiled and said, "The good news is that when we find and arrest Leon, you can testify against him in court and that will ensure he goes to jail for a very long time."
"But what if his mates in the Panthers say he was with them when I saw him? Mum said that's why you haven't arrested anyone yet." At this point, Nick's mum walked into the room, heard what Nick said and saw the two detectives looking at her. "Well," she stammered, blushing, "it's true isn't it?"
"I suppose it is, yes." answered Saunders, "But don't worry Nick. Your testimony and the fingerprints on the gun will be enough evidence to convict Fairbanks." Nick's eyes lit up. "Have you got the gun then?" he asked.
"No. Unfortunately, that's something else we've got to find." Sealey replied.
"So, what's going to happen to us while you're looking for this Fairbanks character and his gun?" asked Nick's mum.
"Well, we're going to put you under the Witness Protection Programme. We'll take you to a safe place until we capture Fairbanks." said Saunders.
"What about school?" asked Nick who immediately felt stupid for sounding like such a swot.

"We'll supply you with a tutor who will teach you at the safe house. It means you can have no contact with any family or friends until we arrest Leon Fairbanks" explained Sealey. Nick couldn't believe this either. Even though he was extremely scared he had been looking forward to making Martin jealous with all of this news but now he couldn't even tell him about it! He began to realise that there is some good for not doing your homework – if he had done the same as Martin at the weekend, he would have been in the house at the weekend and wouldn't have seen anyone shooting at the car.
"Right, let's go then." said Nick's dad.

Chapter eight

After dropping the Knight family off at the safe house, Detectives Sealey and Saunders were driving back to the police station. It was raining and the wipers were squeaking backwards and forwards across the windscreen much to the annoyance of Saunders. "These wipers are driving me mad!" he moaned to Sealey and flicked them onto manual rather than automatic.

Sealey smiled. She and Saunders had only been partners for about six months and he was only now starting to talk to her about everyday things rather than just police work. She realised very quickly that Saunders (she didn't even know his first name yet) loved his work but would rather work alone. She, on the other hand, preferred working with a partner. She enjoyed the camaraderie and the teamwork of having a partner and believed that two brains were better than one. Sealey had only joined this police force six months ago after her old partner died in a gang related shooting. She had been there but had been too late to save her partner.

As Saunders allowed the wipers to do their job, she looked at him and said, "So what do we do now? Go and arrest Fairbanks? We know where he lives."
"No, we can't arrest him, there's not enough evidence, even with the kid's testimony," replied Saunders, shaking his head. "It's Knight's word against Fairbanks'. We need to either catch him trying to harm the kid or find the gun he used to kill the girl."
"Well, I doubt we'll catch him trying to hurt Nick. After all, we've just moved him to a safe house" Sealey pointed out. Saunders nodded, "Find the gun it is then." he replied.

"Where do we start with that task?" enquired Sealey. Saunders thought for a while, going over the options in his head. The gun definitely would not be at Fairbanks' house, he was stupid but not that stupid. What had he done with it? Dumped it? Given it to another gang member to dispose of? It had been almost a week since the murder, the gun could be anywhere by now, even at the bottom of the river that runs through the city.

Saunders rubbed his eyes and sighed. "I don't know. We start at the beginning I suppose. Tomorrow we'll get a team down to the alleyway along Knight's road and see if Fairbanks dumped the gun or part of the gun along it. You never know he might have panicked and just dumped it but I'm not holding my breath on that one." Sealey nodded. She knew Saunders was clutching at straws but she knew he had no choice – how stupid would the police look if they didn't check the alleyway and the gun was eventually found there? Besides, there was a lot of overgrown foliage along that alley, Fairbanks may have thought it a safe place to hide the weapon but, deep down, she knew it was a long shot.

Chapter nine

Leon Fairbanks was sat on his best mate's sofa drinking a beer and smoking a cigarette. He was laughing at something his friend had said but his laugh was stunted by a yawn. Leon was tired. He hadn't slept properly since he killed the girl. He kept replaying the incident over and over in his head and it was worse when he closed his eyes because he could see in every detail, as if it was in slow motion, the girl's face as she flew through the windscreen.

Leon's best mate, the leader of the Panthers – the guy telling jokes now as if he hasn't got a care in the world - had ordered Leon to hurt the girlfriend of Morris Banks, the leader of the Boss Street Crew. He had given Leon the gun and told him where to be and what to do on the day of the shooting. Leon did as he was told. The Panthers had looked after him and supported him through all the tough times in his life, he would do anything for his brothers but he was only supposed to hurt the girl, just like the Boss Crew hurt Freddy, who was still recovering in hospital after his beating at the hands of Morris Banks.

Leon saw the image of the girl as he closed his eyes, how did he know she didn't have a seatbelt on? The silly cow would have lived if she'd been wearing it. Leon kept trying to convince himself that it was her own fault for being careless but he was fooling no-one, he knew he was responsible for her death.

"Hey Leon…..Leon. Oi! You listening to me bruv or what?" Leon's best mate, Charlie Farrell, leader of the Panthers was shouting at him. "Sorry man," Leon sat up and rubbed his eyes again, they were red from fatigue. "I was just thinking."

"Ah man, don't tell me you were thinking about the girl again bruv? Forget it man. It was her fault, she should have been wearing her seatbelt and she shouldn't have been going out with scum like Banks, you know it."

Leon appreciated Charlie's efforts but they fell on deaf ears. This whole thing had surprised Leon; he had learned something about himself. He wasn't as tough as he thought he was.

Since he joined the Panthers at 15, Leon had quickly established himself as a tough guy. He feared no-one and would often end up fighting kids who annoyed him, even if they were older and bigger than him. Despite his hard man reputation he was also extremely loyal to the gang and would do whatever was asked of him from the gang's hierarchy. He shoplifted booze and cigarettes and, as he rose through the ranks of the gang, he went from robbing shops to robbing houses. Even when he was sent to prison he had no regrets in joining the Panthers, they had tried to cover for him but there had been too many witnesses to him beating up that punk from the Boss Street Crew. Leon knew he would be welcomed back into the gang upon his release which proved to be the case and he had risen to the upper echelons of the gang because he had served time for them.

Even when he was given the job of hurting the girl, he took it on without a second's thought. After all, the Boss Crew had it coming for what they had done to Freddy. But now that she was dead, Leon realised that it had had a massive effect on him and he didn't know what to make of it. He still acted the hard guy and only Charlie knew how he really felt but all he wanted to do was get his head down, sleep and wait for it all to go away.

"Mate, forget about it. The girl is dead, you've dumped the gun in the river and the Boss Crew have been given a serious message not to mess with us. It's worked out great for us, bruv. We've all just got to watch our backs for a bit in case Morris Banks tries to get revenge but he won't dare mess with us now, you'll see." Charlie started to laugh and drained the last of his can of lager. He wiped his chin with his sleeve and got up to fetch another can. "You havin' another beer, Leon?"

"What about the boy, Charlie? I'm sure he saw me at the shooting and I know he saw me outside his school."

"I told you not to go to his school, man! That was well stupid. You should've just left him mate, he couldn't have seen you properly with your hood up…"

"But I looked at him!" Leon protested. He knew now that going to the kid's school was a mistake but he wanted to find out where he could find him just in case he needed to pay him a little visit to keep him quiet. Charlie sighed and sat down beside Leon. "Look mate, you've been good to us and we'll help you out. I won't lie to you, the boy could be a problem but we'll sort it, OK? Me and you."

"I've already been to jail because of witnesses, Charlie; I ain't going back there, not for murder. You get me? I ain't going back."

"Woah, mate, mate, mate," Charlie put his arm round Leon's shoulders and waited for Leon to look him in the eye. "You ain't going back to jail, OK. We know where the kid lives and we'll sort it – one way or the other, that kid ain't telling no-one nothing. You trust me don't you mate?"

Leon nodded; he and Charlie would shut the kid up, no problems. "Of course mate." Charlie got up and went into the dingy kitchen. He came back with two beers in his hands but Leon was already fast asleep.

Chapter ten

Martin knocked on Nick's front door for the fourth time. "Where the hell are you?" he said aloud even though there was no-one with him. Nick had been off school for three days now which was unlike him or, should he say, it was unlike Nick's mum. She was really strict when it came to Nick and school – she made him do his homework on time (unlike his own mother) and Martin had once joked that she *might* let Nick have a day off when he died. Nick being off school for three days was unheard of but what was even stranger was the fact that he had not heard anything from Nick since the week before.

Martin had called for Nick every day that week to walk to school with him and the door had never been answered and the driveway had always been empty. Whenever Martin had tried to call Nick's mobile it went to voicemail and Nick had not replied to any of Martin's texts. Martin turned around and scratched his head. "What is going on?" he asked himself. He looked up the road and saw the police crime scene tape around the area of last week's accident. He started to walk towards the tape, he was still gutted that he had missed witnessing the accident as Nick had had a lot of attention at school about it last week but he realised that he was stupid to feel that way. After all, a girl had died – imagine how her family would react if they knew how Martin had felt about missing her death? He was a bit disgusted with himself when he thought of it that way.

Martin reached the crime scene tape which was fluttering in the wind despite remaining quite taut as it wrapped itself around the trees in the grass area opposite Nick's house. He looked at the ground and saw where the grass had been churned up where the girl's car had skidded. He followed these marks until they ended just short of the tree. He looked at the tree, the bark was still missing where the car had hit it and splinters of wood stuck out from the trunk. "Nasty" Martin thought to himself. He allowed his eyes to search around the base of the tree and beyond. It didn't take him long to notice that, despite the police's best efforts to clean the area and recent rain, some blades of grass were still stained with a reddish tinge – the girl's blood. "What a way to go," Martin said to himself as he turned around to walk home.

As he walked, Martin reminisced about the past ten days' events; Nick telling him about his visit to the police station to be interrogated, Nick getting all the attention at school. His thoughts were interrupted as he rounded the corner at the end of Nick's street as he had to step around two young blokes wearing black hoodies and smoking who were walking in the opposite direction to him. They looked tough so Martin moved aside, they didn't even acknowledge him. "You're welcome!" Martin thought to himself as he continued his journey. He stopped. Martin suddenly remembered something else that had happened last week – the guy staring at Nick during music. *He* was wearing a black hoodie and, although Martin didn't really see his face, he seemed to be pretty tough.

Some kind of gut instinct told Martin to turn around and just keep an eye on what the two men did, even though his brain was telling him not to be stupid, it was probably nothing. Martin walked slowly back to the corner of Nick's road where he could see the two men in black walking. He was about to follow more closely but stopped because he soon realised he didn't need to. The two men stopped about three houses short of Nick's house and one of them pointed towards the crime scene tape Martin had been stood at no more than 5 minutes ago. He couldn't be sure but he could have sworn he had heard laughter from the other bloke. Martin ducked down behind a low wall at the end of the road. He watched as the two men carried on walking a short distance before stopping.

 Right outside Nick's house.

They had a quick look around and Martin prayed they had not spotted him. When he dared to look again, he saw the two men walking up Nick's driveway and knock on his door. "What the hell is going on?" Martin thought to himself as he stood up and ran home.

Chapter eleven

Nick lay on his bed staring at the ceiling. Of course, it wasn't *really* his bed, his bed was back home and Nick wished more than anything he was back there too. Nick was bored beyond belief, the novelty of being put in the Witness Protection Program and moving somewhere new had worn off and he did not know what to do with himself. All his stuff was at home; he had only had a short amount of time to gather his things together and was told to only bring the bare minimum that he needed. The first thing Nick had picked up was his mobile phone and charger but even that was proving to be a waste of time because the police and his parents wouldn't let him get in touch with anyone.
Martin had been texting him and leaving him voicemail messages for days now and he sounded more and more worried with each message he left. Nick felt guilty that he couldn't put his mate's mind at rest and tell him he was OK. In fact, he had had quite a few arguments with his parents about it but he never won any of them. Deep down he knew that this whole sorry mess was his fault and they were there because of him and, to be fair, his parents couldn't contact anybody either.

Nick was missing his friends at school too. Surprisingly, he was actually missing school itself! He didn't like his tutor, John Maxwell, who was what Nick would describe as a "boring old fart". His lessons, if they could be called that, were dull and he quite often made Nick do work he had already done at school. When Nick told John that he had done apostrophes for possession at school and understood it, his tutor just shrugged and reasoned, "Well it won't hurt you to do it again." In short, Nick was unhappy and now deeply regretted witnessing the death of the girl outside his house. Her life was over and it seemed to Nick that his was too.

When Nick and his family left their home a week ago, his mind raced as to where they would be relocated. "I hope it's somewhere hot!" he thought to himself, "Florida would be wicked!" Nick remembered that he was expecting a long journey and he had tried to get to sleep in the car but about half an hour later, the car stopped and Detective Saunders had announced that they were at the "safe house."

"We're here already?" Nick had asked in disbelief, "Waste of time me packing my passport then!"

"You've been watching too many American TV shows, Nick" laughed Detective Sealey. "We have to have you fairly close to us in case we need to ask you any more questions or to come and identify Fairbanks when we catch him." Nick appreciated the fact that Sealey had said "when we catch him" rather than "if."

Once they had unpacked in their new home, Nick decided to explore the new place. It didn't take long. It seemed to him that it was about half the size of his actual house. It had two bedrooms rather than the four at his house, one bathroom decorated, if that was the right word, in disgusting yellow tiles, a tiny kitchen and a lounge that didn't even have a flatscreen TV! But the worst thing for Nick was that they didn't even have Sky. Nick found his parents who were still unpacking. "I don't think much of this place."

"Don't start Nick" his dad had replied and the tone of his voice told Nick it was probably best to take that advice. After all, his dad was probably more gutted about the lack of Sky TV than he was. His mum, ever the optimist, simply said, "Anyway, we won't be here for long hopefully because the police will find this Fairbanks person." Nick walked out of the room, "I hope you're right Mum," he thought to himself, "I hope you're right."

Nick's text ringtone went off so he sat himself up on his bed and reached for it. "I bet it's Martin again, wondering where I am" he thought. Nick read the text, it was from Martin, but this one made him shiver and he knew he had to tell his parents about it immediately. He raced downstairs and burst into the lounge where

his parents were watching something on the ancient TV that had a really grainy picture. "You should be in bed" Nick's dad said.
"Look! I just had this from Martin!" Nick exclaimed. His dad looked at him and could see that something had upset his son. He took the phone and read the message. Without saying a word, he passed the phone to Nick's mum who also read the message. "Oh Christ Bill! What do we do?!" Nick's dad thought for a minute, Nick was always impressed at how calm his dad stayed when his mum went into a panic.
"There's nothing we can do now, we're safe where we are at the moment. We wait until morning and we'll call Saunders and Sealey and show them the message." Nick and his mum nodded in agreement. Nick took the phone back from his dad and walked back up the stairs to his room. As he lay down to go to sleep, he had one last look at the message.

```
  Hi mate.   I don't know where you are
but whatever you do DON'T COME BACK!   I
saw that guy who was staring at you at
school knocking on your door today and
  it didn't look like it was a friendly
visit.   There were two of them.   PLEASE
      call me or write back.   Mart.
```

Chapter twelve

As much as he hated to admit it, Detective Saunders was actually glad he had a partner - on this case at least. Sealey was great at dealing with the kid, something he knew he struggled with. He just didn't know how to talk to them, probably because he didn't have kids of his own. They seemed to have their own language these days and used words of which he had no idea what they meant. Anyway, he was glad he was teamed up with Sealey; she seemed perfectly at ease with kids which meant he didn't really have to deal with them. Nevertheless, he did like Nick. He seemed smart, funny and most importantly, sensible. He did as he was told and he obviously understood the difficult situation he was in which was why now he and Sealey were in the lounge of Nick's safe house talking about the message Nick had received last night.

"So who is this Martin then Nick?" Sealey asked.
"He's my best mate from school. Lives not far from me. He's been texting and ringing me since we came here but I haven't replied, honest."
"Like I said – sensible" Saunders thought to himself. He decided that he ought to at least try and talk to the kid. "How much does Martin know about what happened, Nick? Does Leon know who he is?"
"I told Martin about the accident and......"
"It wasn't an accident, Nick. This was intentional. Fairbanks wanted to hurt that girl" corrected Saunders.
"OK, sorry. Martin knows about what I saw and he saw Fairbanks looking at us from the school wall. I don't think he would have seen Mart though because he was just leaning across me."
"We're going to have to interview Martin about what he saw yesterday. Can you give us his address please?" enquired Sealey.
Nick gave the two police officers Mart's address and smiled.
"You're gonna get interrogated at last mate" he thought to himself.

"Right," said Saunders, "we'll go and pay Martin a visit and see if we can work out what Fairbanks is up to. He obviously doesn't know where you are so don't worry, you're still safe here. Thanks for the tea, Mrs Knight. We'll be in touch." Saunders and Sealey walked down the front path and towards their unmarked car. "Are you all right, guv?" Sealey asked.
"Yeah fine. Why?"
"Well there was a kid in that house and I could barely get a word in!" she said, smiling.
"Ha bloody ha! I'm driving." Saunders replied. He got in the car and started to drive towards the address Nick had given him for his friend Martin's house. Saunders thought about what he had just said about finding out what Fairbanks was up to. The truth was he had a fairly good idea what it was and he didn't like it one bit.

Chapter thirteen

As Saunders expected, the interview with Martin did not really shed any new light on the case. The boy did not really see enough of the two men who visited the Knights' house yesterday – it may not have even been Fairbanks but Saunders knew it was pretty likely that it was him. Sealey had had the good idea of going and checking on Nick's house to see if the two men had tried to break in or take anything but the house was fine – no sign of damage or of anyone gaining entry into it.

Both Saunders and Sealey were starting to get increasingly frustrated with the case. It seemed like they knew so much about what had happened but they couldn't prove anything with 100% certainty. The search for the gun had stopped days ago; there was no sign of it anywhere around Nick's neighbourhood. They had considered issuing a warrant to search Fairbanks' house and those of other senior members of the Panthers gang but they knew they wouldn't find either the gun or any other incriminating evidence. The Panthers may appear stupid but they were well organised and would not make the stupid mistake of leaving anything illegal around their homes.

The two detectives sat down at Sealey's desk (which had less clutter on it) with cups of coffee, looked at each other and sighed. "OK," said Sealey, sitting upright in her chair. "Let's break this down. Fairbanks shoots Morris Banks' girlfriend's car. Why?"
"Revenge attack after the Boss Street Crew assaulted Freddy Jackson." replied Saunders.
"Right, but did he mean to kill her? I mean, why shoot the tyre when he could have put a bullet through the driver's side window?" asked Sealey.
"Good point," said Saunders, "perhaps he didn't want to kill her but does it really matter? Either way he was intending on causing her

serious harm." Saunders knew that going over the whole case again could be a waste of time but past experience had shown him that it could bring to light something they hadn't thought of before – sometimes you couldn't see the woods for the trees.

"OK. Fairbanks knows that Nick saw him with the gun and I guess because of this he is worried about him. But why go to his school?" asked Sealey. It appeared that she was going to be the one asking the questions.

"Let's face it, Fairbanks isn't the sharpest tool in the box, in fact he's just a tool." Saunders smiled as he realised that joke had a couple of different meanings. "Who knows why he went to the school? I'm guessing that he wanted to scare Nick or he might just have wanted to know where he could find him if he needed to. What I do know is that going to the school was a mistake because it meant Nick was onto him and Fairbanks had lost the element of surprise. It would have been simpler for him to just ambush Nick one day when he wasn't expecting anything."

Sealey nodded in agreement but she knew they hadn't made any progress yet with this case review. "Next. The gun. Nowhere to be found. All we know is that Fairbanks used one to shoot out the girl's tyre and that he doesn't have a licence to hold a firearm. I think we can safely say that he's dumped it somewhere it'll never be found, like the river, and we can eliminate that line of enquiry."

"Agreed," sighed Saunders, rubbing his temples. He decided it was his turn to lead the review. "So, a man we strongly believe to be Fairbanks visited Nick's house with another guy. Why go there and who was the other guy?"

Sealey thought for a minute and looked through some of the statements, notes and memos that were organised on her desk. "Well our source in the Panthers tells us that Fairbanks has been spending a lot of time with Charlie Farrell lately, maybe it was him?"

"It's a shame that source isn't very high up in the Panthers, we could have nailed Fairbanks by now with that Intel. OK, Farrell is a possibility – Martin's description of his size and dress sense seems to match with Farrell but why would the leader of such a big gang put himself at risk at by accompanying Fairbanks to the house?

Perhaps he and Leon are closer friends than we thought?" Sealey was getting into it now and she tried to answer Saunders' other question. "I think it's pretty obvious why they went to Nick's house. They want him out of the picture. Fairbanks knows that the only thing stopping him from getting away with the murder is Nick. The gun has gone, there were no other witnesses, and he knows Nick is the only one who can put him away for his crime. I wouldn't be surprised if he had another murder planned."

Saunders' eyes widened. "Kill a kid? Fairbanks might be a lot of things but he's not a child killer."

"Maybe not but if it came to killing Nick or going back to prison, I wouldn't be surprised if he decided to get rid of Nick. We know that he had a rough time inside and he won't be too keen on going back." argued Sealey.

The partners sat in silence for a while and let the seriousness of what Sealey had said sink in. Saunders knew that Sealey could well be right. Fairbanks had had a rough time in prison to say the least; unfortunately for him he had been sent to a prison where there were four or five Boss Street Crew members and they soon found out who Leon was. He was beaten once or twice during his imprisonment but the prison warders had told Saunders that Fairbanks was more scared by the *threat* of a beating than the actual act itself. "Imagine that wherever you go in any minute of your day there was a chance that someone could beat you, stab you or worse" one of them had said. No wonder Leon didn't want to go back to prison.

The worst thing was that the powers that be were starting to grow impatient for results on this case and were beginning to apply pressure on Saunders and Sealey to get a conviction. The murder of the girl had made the national press as well as the local papers and although the story had gradually made its way to the latter pages of the national newspapers, the local press were still very much on top of the case and were constantly asking questions of the detectives' superiors. Inevitably, detectives working on other cases were also starting to take the piss which didn't make Saunders any happier.

Just as Sealey was about to suggest lunch and have a break from the case, one such colleague approached Sealey's desk with a smile on his face. It was Andrews, one of the fellow detectives who began the whole mickey taking a few days ago. "Working hard are we? You two have been sat there for over half an hour now having a chat and drinking coffee, I take it you've caught Fairbanks and are waiting for the next case to come along?"
"Oh shut your trap, Max!" Saunders shouted, getting to his feet. He was quite prepared to smack this idiot right in his smug face. Sealey stood up and put her arms between the two policemen. "Ignore him guv, don't rise to the bait, that's what he wants." Andrews walked off smiling and Saunders sat down when an alarm bell went off in his head. "Trap! Bait!" he thought to himself. "Come on, we're going for lunch. I've had an idea." he announced.

Chapter fourteen

Saunders and Sealey drove to the local café in silence. Sealey had asked him what his idea was as soon as they had gotten into the car but Saunders just said that he'd tell her over lunch. She had no idea what he was playing at – one minute he looked as though he wanted to rip Andrews' head off and then the next minute he was as excited as a kid in a toy shop. He clearly wasn't going to say anything until they reached the café so Sealey put her head against the headrest and listened to the drivel coming from the local radio station's adverts.

Saunders had what he thought was a creditable idea but he knew it was a massive risk. He was overcome with excitement when he had the idea but now he wanted the time to let the idea bubble in his head so that he could work out the finer details of how it could work. Fair play to Sealey, he thought, she'd asked him once what his idea was but had left him in silence to think things through when he told her he'd tell her later. He needed this time to think and he appreciated the fact that she was letting him have it – perhaps it wasn't so bad having a partner after all.

The two detectives sat down in the café and ordered their lunch; Sealey had a tuna salad with a bottle of water, Saunders thought he'd reward himself with a large all-day breakfast and a mug of strong tea. Saunders was still thinking while they were waiting for their food so Sealey just busied herself on her phone, checking for messages and if there was anything new and exciting in the App Store. The food arrived and the two started to eat, Sealey was happy to wait to hear this idea and knew that Saunders would take the lead when he was ready; he was clearly thinking hard about something because he kept frowning and biting the skin around his nails which she had never seen him do before. Saunders spoke at last. "OK, I've had an idea. I'm going to tell you it but I don't want you to interrupt me until I've finished because I know what you're going to say and, yes, I know it is risky."

"Mmmm, I don't know if I'm excited or nervous now" smiled Sealey.

"Nervous would probably be your best bet. I think we've both realised that this case has pretty much hit a dead end," began Saunders between mouthfuls of sausage and egg. Sealey nodded. "Well, I think drastic times call for drastic measures and I think I've got a drastic measure that might just work. We strongly suspect that Fairbanks is after Nick Knight so that there are no witnesses to what he did, right?"

"Right" replied Sealey who started to have a strong suspicion as to what the idea was and put down her knife and fork.

"OK, so why don't we let him get Nick? Not really get him but use Nick as bait in order to trap Leon. If we can catch Leon trying to harm or capture Nick then we've got reason to arrest him, we've got a witness to the murder and a motive as to why Leon was after Nick and the motive proves he's guilty of the murder. What do you think?"

Sealey thought for a few minutes without saying anything. Saunders surprised himself because he really wanted to hear her opinion but she had given him time to think so it was only fair he did the same for her. Besides, his lunch was going cold. "You're right, it is a massive risk," Sealey said suddenly, "The problem is if it went wrong and Fairbanks actually gets Nick, it's not just Nick who's in trouble, we are as well. Plus it doesn't prove Leon is guilty, just that he might know who is guilty." Sealey stared at Saunders for a few seconds before sighing, "But I can't see how else we can close this case because, like you said, it's hit a dead end. How are we going to set this trap?"

"I've been thinking about that," answered Saunders, pushing his empty plate forward and picking up his tea. "We know that Fairbanks has visited Nick's house. It wouldn't be a surprise if he goes back there or is watching the house. I bet he's got some kid who's lower down in the gang watching Nick's place right now. I say we bring Nick and his family back home and back to school and go about their normal lives. Leon will probably watch him for a bit to get to know his routines and stuff but it won't be long before he makes a move and tries to get him. All we've got to do is make sure we've got covert surveillance on Nick at all times so that when Leon makes his move, we're there to get him." Sealey had another bit of time to think while she finished off her water.

"I don't know," she said, "it could work but it could go horribly wrong."

"You got a better idea?" asked Saunders. He had expected this kind of reaction, if Sealey had had the idea, he'd be saying exactly the same thing. Sealey had to admit that she hadn't. "Come on," said Saunders, starting to get fired up again. "Nick is a sensible lad, he's got common sense, if he hadn't I wouldn't even think of doing this but he seems like the type of kid who can help us pull this off."

Sealey thought for a while again, Saunders was quite glad she wasn't rushing into this, she might think of something that he hadn't. As the two detectives got up to pay for lunch, Sealey said, "OK, let's go for it but we're gonna have to plan this thing meticulously. Every last detail, alright? Otherwise I'm washing my hands of it."

"Of course, I'm well known for my planning" smiled Saunders.

"Yeah, right! You know what the biggest problem is going to be don't you?" asked Sealey.

"What?"

"Getting Nick's mum to agree to all this."

Chapter fifteen

"Absolutely not. No way! Over my dead body!" Sealey had been right; Nick's mum was putting up a lot of resistance to the plan. The Knight family had sat in silence as Sealey had explained to them that the case had hit a wall and as soon as she outlined the plan to them, Mrs Knight erupted.

"Mum! Calm down! Let's listen to what they've got to say, please?" Nick grabbed his mum's hand and guided her back to her seat. He didn't know how to feel – he was scared and excited. He had a chance to be a real hero and help capture a killer. Imagine how jealous his friends would be and how impressed the girls would be! He might even be on telly or in the newspaper! But, he also knew he could be in serious danger if anything went wrong. At the moment though, the idea of becoming a hero kept all the scary stuff firmly at the back of his mind. His mum sat down and listened as Sealey outlined the plan to Nick's family, she shook her head throughout and kept stroking Nick's hair.

Once Sealey had finished, it became obvious that Mrs Knight hadn't been swayed as she once again refused to give permission for Nick to go through with the plan. "What's the alternative, Detective?" asked Nick's dad. It was the first time he had spoken.
"Well," sighed Saunders who thought he had better say something as it was his idea in the first place. "If we don't do this then the case is effectively closed. The murder will remain unsolved, Fairbanks gets away scot free and you will have the choice of going back home and continually looking over your shoulder or starting a new life away from here."
"But all my friends are here! I don't want to move!" Nick protested.
"Then you can stay at home but there's always that danger that Fairbanks will strike. We can't offer round-the-clock protection for the rest of your life I'm afraid. It would be a huge drain on public

taxes." Saunders knew that he shouldn't be trying to scare them into agreeing to his plan but he also knew that this was their only chance of ending this case. The room went silent for quite some time. Nick's dad broke the silence.
"What do you think, Nick?"
"Bill! You can't seriously be considering this?!" Mrs Knight shouted.
"I'm sorry, love, I don't like it any more than you do but I also don't want this hanging over us for the rest of our lives. Can you imagine living every minute of every day wondering if Nick is safe? Worrying if something had happened to him all the time? I'd rather it ended now and it appears this is the only way."
Nick decided to answer his dad's question before he and his mum started a full-blown slanging match. His initial excitement had dwindled a bit as he had time to think about the consequences should anything go wrong. He was starting to agree with his mum and was going to refuse to do it but his dad's reasoning had made him change his mind once more.

"I don't really want to but I'll do it." His mum started to sob again, realising she was fighting a losing battle. "Mum, I'm sorry but dad's right. I don't want to be worried every time I go out. As long as Fairbanks is out there, I'd feel threatened and I can't have you and dad with me the whole time I'm growing up holding my hand. So," Nick turned to face Saunders and Sealey, "I'll do it but you'd better get him. I don't want to get hurt."
"Come here, son." said Bill Knight who had also started to cry, he had never been prouder of his boy. The Knight family hugged each other tightly; it appeared that Mrs Knight had finally relented to the plan.

Watching this family hold each other brought a tear to Sealey's eyes and even Saunders felt a bit choked up but he gathered himself and spoke to Nick.
"Nick, you're a very brave young man and, in my eyes, you've grown up a lot in the time I've known you. I'm not going to lie to you – this is a very dangerous plan but I know you're up to it and I

promise you that neither Sealey nor I will let anything happen to you. OK?"

Nick looked into Saunders' eyes and could see he meant every word. Nick nodded. "What happens now?" he asked. The two detectives walked towards the door of the safe house. "You stay here for a couple more days while we sort out protection for you and the boring stuff like shift patterns and who is doing what and when. Start packing, the next time you see us, we'll be taking you home."

Chapter sixteen

In less than a week, Nick and his family were back in their own home. Nick was glad to be back and, for the first time, he started to hope that this was the beginning of the end of the nightmare he found himself in.

The Knights had spent the last few days going through the plan in fine detail and meeting the police officers who had been assigned to watch Nick in the daytime and watch the house during the night. Nick was loving it, it was like he was in a film and he felt surprisingly safe considering the predicament he was in. He had really hit it off with Terry, a middle aged policeman who would be watching Nick every other day. Terry was funny and knew how to put Nick at ease, he told him that he had done this kind of protection before and they had caught the offender within a week. Nick hoped that the same thing would happen again with Leon Fairbanks.

The first few days back living his normal life were uneventful for Nick. He was desperate to tell people at school why he had been off for so long and what was happening but Saunders had ordered him not to tell anyone in case the Panthers got wind of it and warned Leon. Of course, Nick's head teacher had been informed but the staff was also instructed not to mention anything regarding Nick's absence. While Nick was in school, the officers guarding him kept a discreet distance outside the school. They were watching for any sign of either Fairbanks or any known member of the Panthers loitering around the school. Terry had told Nick it was very boring but it had to be done. Occasionally Terry liked to have a walk around the perimeter of the school just to stretch his legs but every time Nick spotted him from a window on the first floor of the school, he was reading a paper or eating crisps.

Martin was driving Nick mad. He knew something was up and kept pestering him to tell all about where he had been while he was off school. To be honest, Nick was close to telling Martin what was going on because, to be fair, Martin had warned him about the two Panthers who visited his house. Nick felt like he owed him one but he also knew that Martin was about as good at keeping secrets as Lady Gaga is at dressing normally. "Come on mate. What's going on? Please tell me, I won't tell anyone else, I swear!" pleaded Martin. Nick looked around.

"I can't mate. Listen, give me a couple of days and I'll tell you but we need to be on our own when I tell you."

"That's OK; we can find a place to go where you can tell me, easy."

"It won't be as easy as you think," Nick said cryptically.

"What? Why? Oh I want to know even more now!"

"Sorry mate, you're going to have to wait, otherwise I won't tell you anything at all."

"OK, I'll wait" groaned Martin and, for once, he changed the subject.

After tea each evening, the officer or officers who had been watching Nick all day would give the Knights a debriefing on the day. Sometimes Saunders or Sealey would lead the debriefing but it was usually just the officers who had been on duty. Normally there was nothing to report and the week to capture Fairbanks that Nick and Terry had been hoping for had passed. The debrief on day 9 though threw up some worrying news. The debrief was led by Ali, another officer who had watched Nick that day. Normally Terry and Ali would do alternate days, Nick liked Ali but he didn't make the same effort to talk to Nick like Terry did.

"OK. Debrief, Day 9." Ali began, "We have a development. Over the past 3 days Terry and I have spotted the same few lads walking around this street and around Nick's school. We haven't said anything as it could have just been a coincidence. However, Terry took some photos of the boys yesterday and sent them to Detective Sealey, she has run a check on them and they are known members of the Panthers."

"Oh God!" whispered Nick's mum. Nick felt sick.

"We sent another officer to follow the boys and it didn't take her long to see the lads meet up with Fairbanks. In fact, he was just around the corner."

"Why would Fairbanks put himself near Nick? It's a bit risky isn't it?" asked Nick's dad.

"Fairbanks is the only one who knows what Nick looks like. He's got to be close in case they start watching the wrong kid."

"What does all this mean, Ali?" enquired Bill Knight.

"It looks like they're watching Nick, trying to work out his habits. Where he'll be at different times of the day and stuff like that. Once they feed back Nick's routine to Fairbanks and his cronies, they'll try and figure out when he's most vulnerable and try and lift him. That's my theory anyway"

"Lift me?" asked Nick.

"Kidnap you mate," Ali replied. Nick appreciated Ali's honesty but he felt worse now than he ever had before. "The good news is that it doesn't look like they know that Nick has surveillance on him so, all being well, they'll make a move and we'll be able to get them as they try and get Nick."

"Yeah, all being well!" scoffed Nick's mum as she stormed out of the room. She was angry at herself for giving in to letting Nick go through with this ridiculous plan.

Ali watched her go and continued. "It doesn't look like they're going to act anytime soon but you never know so you need to be really switched on now Nick, OK?"

"OK."

After Ali had debriefed the night time surveillance officers and left, Nick decided that he wasn't going to do his homework as he had other things on his mind that were more important than sub-clauses and complex sentences. His dad wrote him a note for his teacher that Nick would not be handing his homework in tomorrow and Nick went to bed. The house had been very quiet since Ali left. Nick's mum had gone into a cleaning frenzy and every surface was now spotless. Nick's dad had tried to cheer Nick up but Nick could sense the tension in his father as they played on the PS3 together.

Nick lay down and thought about the idea of being kidnapped. It scared the life out of him but he did make one decision. Tomorrow he would tell Martin what was going on. It comforted him to know that, should anything go wrong, Martin would know what he had been through and may even be able to help in some way. Nick rolled the panic alarm that Saunders had given him in his hand. He had a nasty feeling he might have to use it pretty soon.

Chapter seventeen

Nick was determined to tell Martin everything that was going on the next day and overnight he had worked out when he would be able to tell him. Nick had to follow the same route to and from school every day. Sealey explained that this was for two reasons: 1 – it meant the police would know where Nick was at any time on his journey should they lose him somehow and 2 – it would make it easier for Fairbanks and the Panthers to track Nick and lure them into trying to get him. Nick decided that he would tell Martin on the way home from school as they walked through the park. It was Terry's turn to watch him today and he always gave Nick a bit of space when walking to and from school because he didn't want anyone to notice him.

The time came for Nick to tell Martin what was happening and he actually felt nervous about it but he didn't really know why. Martin had been pretty good over the past few days; he had hardly nagged Nick to tell him what was happening.

As they entered the park, Nick had a quick look round to see where Terry was, he was about 80 yards behind the two boys, well out of ear-shot. "Listen mate, I'm gonna tell you what's been happening but you've got to promise you won't tell anyone." Nick started.

"I won't Nick, I promise." Nick could hear the excitement in Martin's voice.

"I mean it Mart, this is serious. You've got to swear that you'll keep quiet – my life is at stake here." Martin stopped walking and looked at Nick open-mouthed. "Keep walking, we need to keep our distance." Nick commanded.

"What? Who from?"

"Keep walking and I'll tell you" hissed Nick. The two boys began walking through the park and Nick began to tell Martin everything from when he disappeared for a few weeks. Unusually, Martin did not interrupt once; he was too stunned to ask questions. He didn't even realise he was walking, his whole focus was on what his friend was telling him and he soon began to realise that he was glad that he hadn't witnessed the car crash after all.

The boys followed the path through the park and reached a T-junction, they turned 90° to their left. The path ran parallel to a stream on their right and a large row of hedges to their left meaning they were unsighted to Terry. Nick had never realised this but he was about to find out.

He was just about to tell Martin about the police surveillance he was getting when they heard footsteps quickly approaching them from behind. Before either of them had a chance to look behind, a man in a hooded top grabbed Martin and continued running down the path away from Nick. "Help! Nick! Help!" Martin called as the man ran around the corner with Martin over his shoulder in a kind of fireman's lift. Nick froze, "They've snatched Martin instead of me!" he thought to himself. From behind, the two boys would have looked alike. "TERRY!" Nick screamed but Terry was already running as he rounded the corner. Nick pointed, "Quick, they've taken Martin!" Terry stopped, already out of breath, "I heard a cry for help. Thank God it's not you, Nick. Listen, stay right here. Someone will be along for you in a minute or two. I'll go after Martin." As he started running off, Nick could see Terry speaking into his walkie-talkie.

Nick felt awful, this was all his fault. He had never dreamed this would happen – he had thought he was the only one in danger, possibly his parents too. He hadn't even considered Martin being in harm's way even though he spends more time with him in public than he does with his mum and dad. Suddenly, he heard a rustling from the hedges behind him to his left. Nick spun around and there in front of him was a face he never wanted to see again. "So, your name's Nick is it?" Leon Fairbanks grinned.

Chapter eighteen

Terry was getting tired and he'd only been running for about a minute, more worryingly, he still hadn't caught sight of the man who had snatched Martin. "I should be able to catch a guy carrying a kid!" he thought to himself. As he rounded a corner he stopped in his tracks. There, sitting on the grass, looking petrified was Martin. Terry ran over. "Are you all right mate?"
"I...I think so." Martin stammered, "He just dropped me here and legged it."
"He probably realised he had the wrong….." Terry cut himself short. "Nick!" Terry ran off in the direction he had come from with a horrible feeling in the pit of his stomach. Martin was running alongside him, "What? What's the matter with Nick?" he asked as they ran but Terry didn't answer, he just wanted to get back to Nick.
"What's that noise?" Martin enquired. Terry had heard it too, he knew what it was and it made him feel sick with worry.

Sure enough, as they approached where they had left Nick, in the middle of the path was the source of the noise. The unmistakeable sound of a panic alarm. Terry picked it up, breathing heavily, "Saunders is going to kill me" he thought to himself.

Chapter nineteen

"What the bloody hell happened?" Terry winced. He had barely got through the door and Saunders was already firing questions at him. Sealey followed the two men in with three cups of tea. The three of them sat down and looked at each other. Each one of them had a reason to panic but they also knew that panicking wouldn't solve the problem and get Nick back. Terry went through exactly what happened, leaving out no details. After he'd finished, Sealey simply said, "Well, I guess we underestimated the Panthers. They're obviously much better organised than we thought. They knew we were watching Nick and planned a way of getting him without getting caught themselves."
"I'd be surprised if it was Fairbanks that came up with the plan," sighed Saunders, "but you're right. They've outwitted us."
"What are we going to do?" asked Terry. There was silence as they all thought what their options were. Saunders was not expecting a ransom note; they hadn't kidnapped Nick for money, they'd done it to shut him up which meant that they probably didn't have much time. Sealey spoke first. "Why don't we start checking out known Panthers' hide-outs? They've got to have taken Nick somewhere?"

Saunders nodded. "OK, get a team of officers to do that but I'm not holding much hope on that one – we don't know all of their hide-outs but you never know." He looked at Terry and Sealey and exhaled, "Who wants to tell Nick's parents?" Another silence but Saunders spoke up within seconds. "I'll do it; this was all my stupid idea after all." Sealey had never seen him looking so worried and angry and she suspected much of the anger wasn't aimed at Terry or even Fairbanks but at himself for putting Nick in danger in the first place.

Terry pulled out his mobile and held it up, "I'm just gonna phone the wife, tell her I'll be back late tonight." Saunders stared at Terry.

There was an idea forming in the back of his mind but he couldn't quite get it to come forward. He watched as Terry dialled his number and waited for his wife to answer. In a flash, it hit him, "His mobile!" Saunders exclaimed. "Terry, you might just have redeemed yourself!" and with that, he shot out of the room with Sealey close behind.

Chapter twenty

Sealey struggled to keep up with her partner as he strode off and took the stairs two at a time. "Saunders wait! What's the idea?" They stopped on a landing in the stairwell. Saunders looked at Sealey, "We need to pray that Nick had his mobile with him when he was taken. If he did, we can trace it and find out where he is." Sealey smiled, she knew that this was probably their only hope of finding Nick before anything happened to him. "OK, you run a trace on his phone. I'm going to see Martin."
"What for?" asked Saunders.
"I'm gonna talk to him about what happened and make sure he doesn't blab about it to everybody. Then I'm going to see Nick's parents."
"Do you want me to come?" Saunders thought it really should be him to tell Nick's parents that their son had been taken.
Sealey shook her head, "No. I'm not going to tell them yet. With a bit of luck we'll have him back before they find out."
"That's a bit risky isn't it?" said Saunders.
Sealey shrugged as she started back down the stairs. "We're in enough trouble as it is. One more cock-up won't make any difference! Call me when you find his phone!"
"Good luck!" Saunders shouted as she disappeared down the stairs, "Something tells me we're going to need it," he said to himself.

Chapter twenty one

Nick was breathing heavily, not because he'd been running; he hadn't had the chance to run, Fairbanks had grabbed him quickly and run out the back of the park through the woods where very few people were. He was breathing heavily because he was panicking. There was a car waiting for them when they got out of the woods. The driver got out and put a sack over Nick's head, they then shoved him down in the foot well in the back of the car. Nick was too frightened to shout for help, he knew no-one would hear him anyway – whoever was driving had the stereo on very loud – just like the girl who was killed in Nick's street. That had only been about six weeks ago but for Nick it seemed like years.

The car eventually stopped and Nick was dragged out of the car and taken into a building where they sat him down on an uncomfortable wooden chair and tied his arms behind the chair. They also tied something around the sack where his mouth was to stop him screaming. Without uttering a word, they walked back out the room and left Nick alone.

A million thoughts raced through Nick's mind. Where am I? What am I going to do? What are they going to do to me? Will I see my family or Martin again? The answer to all of the questions was "I don't know" and Nick knew that things were looking bleak for him. He forced himself to calm down by breathing as deeply and as controlled as he could with a sack over his head. Eventually, he felt himself calm down and decided to start thinking positively.

Nick had never forgotten what Sealey had said to him when they first interviewed him; she had said he was observant and would make a good detective. He knew he couldn't see anything but perhaps he could get some clues as to where he might be. Nick listened really carefully, he could hear muffled voices from another room, he could only make out two different voices but that didn't mean there weren't more Panthers around. Nick remembered that when they left him on this chair the sound of the door shutting had echoed. He realised that it's true that your other senses are heightened when you can't see. He stamped his foot on the floor, "Definitely a concrete floor," he thought to himself. The sound of the stamp also echoed, Nick thought he might be in a garage or something. He could feel the panic start to rise in him again, "OK, I know what kind of room I'm in and that there's at least two other people around, that's not going to help me get out of here is it?" he thought to himself. He started to wriggle his hands to try and get free of the rope that tied him to the chair but it was pretty tight and hurt his wrists. He stopped struggling and sat still, "Oh crap!" he thought to himself.

Chapter twenty two

"Malcolm!" Saunders burst into the office of Malcolm Armitage, the police force's techno-boffin. Of course, this wasn't his official title but all the officers knew that if there was something needing doing that involved gadgets; Malcolm was the man to ask. "I need a massive favour from you, mate." Saunders had always gotten on well with Malcolm, in fact he was one of the few people he addressed by his first name, he didn't even do that with Sealey yet and she was his partner.

"What's up this time, Mike? Got some dodgy sites on your computer that need erasing?" quipped Armitage, chuckling at his own joke.

"No, I need to track a mobile phone." Armitage stopped laughing. "What? Have you got permission for that?"

"Mmmm not as such, no," admitted Saunders. He knew what he was asking of Armitage was highly irregular – there were proper procedures to go through to get a phone tracked but he knew he didn't have time for all that. Besides which if he went through the proper channels, he'd have to admit that his plan hadn't worked and he'd be in serious trouble. Deep down, Saunders knew he was in serious trouble anyway but he thought that if he managed to get Nick back and arrest Fairbanks and maybe some other Panthers too, he'd be in less trouble than he was in right now.

"Look mate, I'm in serious bother here. I could lose my job and a young lad could be badly hurt, killed even. If you don't track his phone I've got no way of finding him and stopping that from happening. Please, I'm desperate, I'll owe you one." Saunders almost felt bad for resorting to emotional blackmail but he knew it was the only way he'd get Armitage to risk his own job for him. Armitage stared at him for what seemed like minutes; Saunders was almost holding his breath willing him to make up his mind. Eventually, Armitage let out a loud sigh, "You'll owe me more than one mate. What's the number?"

Chapter twenty three

Nick hated waiting around for Fairbanks and his cronies to come back. It was like being in the dentist waiting room but a thousand times worse and possibly a thousand times more painful too. Suddenly a thought hit him like a hammer – "I just stamped my feet! They haven't tied my feet! I can walk. If this is a garage, I might be able to find the door and push it open and, with a bit of luck, someone might see me and help me!" He knew that he would need a lot of luck for this escape plan to work but it was his only hope.

"The door should be straight in front of me, just be quiet and hope they don't come and check on me," he thought to himself. Nick stood up tentatively and took a deep breath, it was strange not being able to see anything. Carrying the chair behind him, he started to take big but slow steps forward, deliberately raising his knees high in case he kicked anything that might be on the floor. Nick had no idea if he was heading for the door or not and it seemed to take ages before he finally walked into something.

Nick felt the surface with his foot – it was a brick wall. "Damn!" he thought to himself. He started to feel around with his left foot and eventually felt it hit another surface when he stretched to his left. He turned and walked towards it. After a couple of steps he reached the surface and gave it a gentle tap with his foot; a metallic clang. Nick's heart beat even faster, "Please be unlocked" he prayed as he turned around and put the chair against what he hoped was a garage door.

Slowly, Nick started to push back against the door. Sure enough the door started to lift upwards and although he was lifting it slowly the door seemed to be making a hell of a noise as he opened it. He stopped for a second to let the noise dissipate and listen out to see if anyone was coming. Nothing. Again, Nick started pushing backwards but the door started to scrape against the chair which added to the noise. He stopped again and turned around. Stooping low, Nick started to push the door further upwards using his head, the sack actually cushioning his head against the door. Nick could see light coming through the sack, "Yes! Keep going, you're almost there!" he thought to himself. At that moment, the worst possible thing happened. Nick's mobile started ringing.

Chapter twenty four

"Well the bad news is he's not answering his phone, the good news is it is switched on so it's transmitting," explained Malcolm Armitage as he hung up the phone. Saunders nodded his head, relieved that something was going his way. "Does that mean you can find out where he is?"
"I should be able to, yes," nodded Armitage, "but before I do, I want to make it very clear that if all this goes tits up, I don't want any flak coming my way. Deal?"
"Deal. Thanks Malcolm and don't worry, I'll get him back."
Armitage started tapping away at his computer terminal; he didn't explain to Saunders what he was doing because he knew he wouldn't understand. After a few minutes, he turned and said, "OK, I can't give you an exact address because the signal isn't that strong but I can tell you he's somewhere along Tennyson Avenue."
"Malcolm, you're a star. Thanks again mate, I'll keep you posted." Saunders ran back out of Armitage's office. "Just get the lad back!" yelled Armitage.

"No! Not now!" Nick pleaded as he tried to do something about his phone. He couldn't turn it off because his hands were tied and he couldn't even smash it because it was in his pocket. After what seemed an eternity, the phone stopped ringing but Nick knew it was too late, he could hear voices approaching the other end of the room. He started pushing the door open again, not caring about the noise it made this time.

"What the….? Hey! Get back here you little sod!" The voice got louder as the person it belonged to approached Nick. He grabbed Nick and pulled him roughly back to the other end of the room where he was forced to sit again. "Leon you muppet, you didn't lock the garage door!" the voice bellowed.
"What?" Nick sensed that Fairbanks had come back into the garage.

"You didn't lock the bloody door! I just came in here because I heard some music or something and the kid was half way out the bloody door!"
"OK Charlie, calm down! Sorry. Wait a minute; you heard music coming from in here?"
"I dunno, it was very faint, it was him scuffling about I heard more I think. Check him; he must have a mobile on him or something."
Nick was made to stand up and he could feel Leon's hands, this murderer's hands, moving over his body checking for anything he had. It didn't take long for him to find the mobile. "Yep, 1 missed call, it was his phone. What shall we do with this?"
"Sling it and then lock that door will ya?" ordered Charlie Farrell. Leon walked over to the garage door, opened it a little and threw the phone out into the front garden, he'd deal with it later when they were tidying things up – no-one would see it – the grass was knee high. Leon often joked that the garden could hide an actual panther. He closed the garage door and double-checked it was locked. Nick heard another chair being pulled in front of him, "Right then, Nick, what are we going to do with you?"

Chapter twenty five

"Sealey! Where are you?" Saunders was driving quite recklessly out of the police station as well as talking on the phone. He hadn't even put his seatbelt on yet but he knew time was of the essence. "OK, stay there; I'm coming to pick you up. We've got a lead. Wait!" Saunders realised he hadn't quite finished talking to Sealey yet. "Have you told her anything?" Sealey gave him the answer he wanted. "Good, OK, keep it like that. I'll be there in 10."
Seven minutes later, Saunders screeched to a halt outside Nick's house. Sealey was already there waiting for him. "Christ you didn't waste any time!" she said as she clambered into the car.
"Buckle up, I'll explain on the way." Sealey tried her best to concentrate on what Saunders was telling her while she held on for dear life. She thought the door handle was going to come off in her hand as Saunders thrashed the car into a right hand turn. "OK," she stammered, "we know he's in Tennyson Avenue. How are we going to find him?"
"I've thought about that." Saunders slowed the car down as they entered Tennyson Avenue. "We'll drive along the road and give Control the registration plates of the cars parked on the drives. Hopefully one of them will come up as a known Panthers' car." Sealey nodded, impressed. "Good thinking. Then what?"
"Why do I have to come up with all the ideas?" snapped Saunders, "We'll cross that bridge when we come to it."

Saunders drove slowly along the road while Sealey took note of the number plates. Eventually, on the third batch of plates given to Control, came a breakthrough. "Car registration BS07 MSV is an uninsured vehicle. It belongs to a Mr C. Farrell"
"YES!" shouted Saunders. "That's our house, that's where Nick is." The two detectives sat and watched the house for a while, there didn't seem to be much movement – no noise from a stereo, no-one appearing at a window. "I wonder whose house this is because

it's not Farrell's?" asked Saunders. Sealey nodded and then another thought struck her. "Don't shout but if we're going in there, we really should have a warrant."
Saunders nodded, "I know, I realised that on the way here but sod it, we haven't got the time. For all we know they could have hurt Nick already. Besides, somebody once said to me 'We're in enough trouble as it is, one more cock up won't make any difference'"
Sealey smiled, "Well they are very wise words. OK, let's get closer to the house; we might be able to hear something."

The pair got out of the car and walked nonchalantly past the house, it was early evening but it was still light and they didn't want to attract attention by sneaking up to the house. Saunders had an idea, "Let's walk past again, I'm gonna try something." They turned around and made their way back towards the house, as they approached it, Saunders got out his phone and dialled Nick's number. Sure enough, the sound of a phone ringing came from somewhere in the jungle outside the house. He hung up straight away before anyone inside the house also heard it. They continued walking, "Well," sighed Sealey, "he's in there somewhere. Let's hope he's still in one piece."

Chapter twenty six

Nick blinked rapidly as the bag was pulled off his head. There in front of him was Fairbanks and he'd already worked out the other one must be Charlie. The three just stared at each other for a while. Nick listened for any other voices; it seemed that it was just these two here with him as he couldn't hear anything else coming from in the house. He didn't know if this was a good or a bad thing.

Charlie was waiting for Leon to make the first move because he assumed he had plans for the kid.

Leon on the other hand was starting to panic. When he had asked Nick what they were going to do with him, he had intended it to sound menacing but he quickly realised that he didn't actually know what to do next – could he really hurt this little kid? Taking off the bag made things worse because the kid looked terrified.

"Come on Leon, get on with it" Farrell barked. Fairbanks decided to be honest with Nick even if it meant losing face in front of Charlie. "Look, Nick, I'm sure you can understand my situation here. I'm not a killer alright? The girl wasn't supposed to have died. The silly cow should have had her seatbelt on but she didn't and she's dead."
"Leon, just get on with it!" ordered Farrell.
"Look Charlie, I'll deal with him but I'm doing it my way OK? You wanna deal with it, then be my guest." Farrell held his hands in the air; he wasn't going to hurt the kid. He was many things but he knew he wasn't a child killer, he felt bad enough being involved in all this but he knew he owed Leon for not grassing him up in the past. Fairbanks looked back at Nick who was breathing very quickly, his eyes wide. "Then I saw you looking at me. You were at the wrong place at the wrong time, Nick, know what I mean? If you hadn't have seen me, we wouldn't be here right now. But you did and here we are."

"Look, just let me go please!" Nick pleaded, "I won't tell anyone anything about this or what I saw you do, I promise. Let me go and I'll get on with my life and you can get on with yours." Fairbanks shook his head and looked at the floor.

"If only it was that simple mate. Fact is, you've already told the police about me haven't you? I ain't going back to jail Nick, you understand? And in my eyes there's only person alive who can put me back in jail." Fairbanks paused and looked up at Nick. "And that person is you."

Chapter twenty seven

Saunders and Sealey returned to their car and sat and thought about what their next move was going to be. Saunders spoke first, "Look, I'm not wasting any more time waiting for something to happen. We need to radio in for some back-up and get in there." "Agreed," Sealey nodded, "and I think I know how we can get in." "How?" enquired Saunders. Sealey explained her plan to her partner, she caught herself smiling as she outlined her idea; she had no idea where the plan came from but it was so strange it might just work. "And you reckon that'll work do you?" Saunders asked after hearing of Sealey's idea but he couldn't help smiling at the thought too.
"The Lord works in mysterious ways, Saunders. Come on, let's give it a go." Saunders called in for back-up and then the two detectives spent a minute or two doing their best to smarten up their appearance.

Nick really was terrified now. Why did he ever agree to Saunders' plan to use him as bait? His mum was right, he should have said no and gone and moved somewhere else or something. Thinking about his mum made Nick even more scared – 'will I ever see her again?' he thought to himself. The way things were looking the answer was "No".

Charlie had left the garage and gone back into the house. He returned moments later with a large knife and handed it to Fairbanks. "Here you are mate. Enough of the heart to heart, eh. Just get it over and done with and then we can forget the whole thing, yeah?" Nick started to shuffle backwards on the chair he was still tied to in a futile attempt to get away. "Don't be stupid kid;" said Farrell, "you ain't going nowhere like that. Come on Leon, do what you've gotta do." Leon took the knife and stared at it. It felt so heavy in his hand. He looked at Nick who had started to cry which made the knife seem even heavier.

Nick knew he had to stop this but how? He realised that his only chance was to try and talk his way out of it. It probably wouldn't work but it might buy him a bit more time for something to happen. "Wait!" he sniffed, forcing himself to stop crying. "You just said you're not a killer. OK, the girl's death was an accident but if you do this," he swallowed, looking at the knife. "If you do this, you definitely will be a killer." There was no response from Fairbanks, he just continued to turn the knife over and over in his hand but Nick could tell he was listening. Nick's mind seemed to be screaming at him 'Keep talking, say anything, he might change his mind!'

"Look, Leon. The police do know about you and they're gonna find you sooner or later. Do you wanna be charged with one murder or two?"

"Don't listen to him, Leon." Farrell interrupted. "They ain't gonna find you, we'll protect you. Anyway, even if they do get you, they'll have no proof at all that you killed the girl as long as you get rid of this mouthy kid. Now get on with it!" he shouted. Suddenly there was a loud knock on the front door and both men stood bolt upright and looked at each other.

Chapter twenty eight

The garage was silent. The knock on the door had shocked everyone but Nick was first to react. "HEL…….!" Before he had a chance to scream for help, Farrell had clamped his hand over Nick's mouth and hit him hard around the head. "Ssshhhhh!" he hissed in Nick's ear. "Stay quiet or I'll get that knife and kill you right now." Nick quietened down but Farrell kept his hand firmly over his mouth. "Who the hell is that?" Leon whispered.
"I don't bloody know!" replied Farrell. "Just ignore it and they'll go away." Leon hoped that Charlie was right. Nobody in the garage moved. The knocking continued. It wasn't a repeated knock, there was a pause but each time the knock came it got louder and more insistent. "Go and see who it is, Charlie will ya?" pleaded Fairbanks. "I can't go, look at me, I'm a mess." Farrell stared at his mate. "Bloody hell Leon, I always thought you were a tough guy. Come here then and keep this kid quiet. If you let him scream, I'll be using that knife on both of you!" Leon put the knife in his back pocket and replaced Charlie's hand with his over Nick's mouth. Still the knocks came. Charlie stormed out of the garage and opened the front door. "WHAT?!" he shouted.

In front of him were two smartly dressed people, a man and a woman, both of whom smiled at him despite the fact he had just yelled at them. "Good evening, sir, sorry to disturb you on this beautiful evening." said the woman calmly.
"Yeah, yeah, what do you want?" Farrell asked impatiently.
"Have you ever thought about how beautiful our world is, sir? Or about our Lord who created it?"
"Oh Christ! Are you Jehovah's Witnesses?"
The woman nodded, "We are, sir and we'd like to come in and talk to you about our Lord the Creator."
"You're havin' a laugh ain't ya? Now get lost!" Farrell screamed at the pair. He began to slam the door in their faces but the man

quickly stepped forward and jammed his foot in the door. Farrell stared at him, stunned. "We really do insist on coming inside and talking to you, sir," growled the man who then head-butted Charlie Farrell square on the nose.

Farrell staggered backwards and landed on the hallway floor clutching his nose. Through tear-filled eyes he could see the man and the woman enter the house. Before he had a chance to shout anything the man was upon him, clasping his hand over Charlie's mouth, making it almost impossible for him to breathe. The woman went behind Farrell and handcuffed his hands behind his back. "Let me explain the situation to you, son," the man growled in his ear. "I've got a strong suspicion you've got a young lad called Nick somewhere in this pit. We want to find him, OK? Now, if you're a good boy and help us out, you might not be in as much trouble as you think. Understand?" Saunders could sense that Farrell was having trouble breathing but he kept his hand clasped tight as a way of helping him make his mind up more quickly. Farrell nodded.

"OK. Now, I'll let go of your gob but if you make any noise the hand goes back on for longer. Nod if you understand." Farrell nodded. Saunders slowly took his hand away. "Good," whispered Saunders, "now. Show my colleague behind you how many more of you are in this place. Don't talk, just hold up your fingers." Farrell did as he was told. Saunders looked at Sealey who held up one finger. "So there's just you and one other scumbag here, right?" Farrell nodded. "Good. Do either of you have any weapons?" Farrell shook his head. "Good. Very quietly now, I want you to tell me where this other guy and Nick are." Farrell stared at this copper, pure hatred in his eyes. He was still finding it hard to breathe and see clearly, his nose was almost certainly broken. Blood was pouring into his mouth as he continued to gulp in air. Eventually, he spat out a mouthful of blood at the copper's feet and whispered, "Der in da garudge, pig."

Chapter twenty nine

Leon Fairbanks was beginning to panic even more. Charlie seemed to be taking ages but he knew that if he called for him, Charlie would go mad at him and he couldn't go and check what was going on because the kid would start screaming. "Come on Charlie!" he whispered to himself.

Saunders quickly moved Farrell into the lounge and sat him on the floor. Without talking, Sealey quickly uncuffed one of Farrell's hands and tied him to a radiator pipe. Saunders then gave her his handcuffs and she tied Farrell's other hand to the opposing radiator pipe. Saunders looked at Sealey and whispered, "He's gonna start shouting the place down if we leave the room. Are you OK to watch him until back-up arrives?"
Sealey nodded, "I'll keep him quiet, don't worry. He makes a sound and there's an old sock on the floor here that's gonna get shoved down his throat." Saunders smiled at Sealey and then squatted down in front of Farrell, "You stay quiet mate. Believe me; you don't want to annoy her." He winked at Farrell and playfully slapped his face. He went to leave the lounge but Sealey stopped him. "Saunders, be careful OK?" He nodded and left the room.

Saunders tiptoed along the hallway and into the kitchen trying to make as little noise as possible. He had a quick search through the kitchen drawers for anything that could be used as a weapon; the only thing he could find was a rolling pin. Taking it, he headed to the door in the corner of the kitchen which he presumed to be an internal door to the garage. He put his ear to the door but could only make out a faint shuffling of feet on concrete. Slowly putting his hand on the door handle with his left hand and clutching the rolling pin firmly with the other, Saunders took a deep breath and decided the best thing to do was to storm in there and hopefully scare Fairbanks into giving himself up.

Leon Fairbanks jumped backwards as Saunders burst through the door. "Give it up, Fairbanks. It's over!" shouted Saunders.
Leon held his hands out in front of him as if they were a barrier between him and this man. "Oh Christ! Not you again!"
"I didn't think you'd remember me, Leon! I'm touched!" Leon decided there was no way he was going to show any weakness in front this copper. If he was going down, he was going down fighting but he noticed Saunders was holding a rolling pin which could do some damage. "Some copper. What's with the rolling pin?" he sneered.
"Times are hard, Leon," shrugged Saunders who started to walk towards Leon. "Come to the station with me nice and quietly, yeah? You don't wanna end up like your mate out there do you?"
"What? Where's Charlie?"
"Charlie? You mean that's Charlie Farrell tied up out there with a broken nose and crying like a baby? I've gotta tell you Leon, that's just about made my day." Saunders continued to slowly advance on Leon who was stepping back towards the garage doors as they talked. "I mean I get to arrest a killer and the leader of the Panthers all in one day? My boss is gonna love me!"
Nick was behind both men now and he watched in silence as Saunders started to back Fairbanks into the corner of the garage. He couldn't take his eyes of Fairbanks' face; it was completely different to the one he looked at less than 10 minutes ago.

Leon was angry at himself for giving away who Charlie was but he had a plan, he just needed to get the copper closer to him. Leon eventually found himself with his back to the wall but he wasn't scared anymore. He knew what he had to do and he felt a lot better about killing a copper than he did about killing a kid. "Yeah, yeah. Keep laughing pig. I ain't going anywhere with you." Slowly, hoping that the copper wouldn't notice, he lowered his right hand to his side and started to reach behind him. Watching this, Nick realised what was about to happen. "He's got a knife!" he shouted. Fairbanks had no choice now; he grabbed the knife and lunged forward at the copper. Saunders sidestepped this attack and smacked Fairbanks across the cheek with the rolling pin. Nick saw spit, blood and even a few teeth fly out of Leon's mouth as he took the blow. Within seconds, Saunders brought the rolling pin down hard on Leon's hand and he dropped the knife. Kicking the knife away, Saunders rolled Leon Fairbanks onto his front and brought his hands behind his back. He then sat on Leon's back and held his hands in place. "Leon Fairbanks, I'm arresting you on charges of murder, kidnap and intent to harm a witness. You do not have to say anything. But it may harm your defence if you do not mention when questioned something which you later rely on in court. Anything you do say may be given in evidence." Saunders turned and looked at Nick. "You OK Nick? Have they hurt you?" Nick shook his head and said "No, I'm fine but I'm glad you turned up because that knife was meant for me." Saunders nodded and replied, "I gathered that. Sealey!" he shouted, "Bring a pair of those cuffs in here please. Charlie Farrell can scream and shout as much as he wants now!"

Sealey quickly entered the garage and handed the cuffs to Saunders who put them on Leon Fairbanks. Sealey then went over and untied Nick from the chair. Tears had stuck some of his hair to his face and she tenderly brushed his hair from his cheeks and smiled at him. "Are you OK, Nick?"
"I'm fine, thanks." Nick replied.
"You were right, Sealey. He is observant, if he hadn't warned me about the knife, I could be on that floor now instead of that scumbag. Thanks Nick." Saunders smiled at Nick and ruffled his hair.
"No problem," Nick replied, "and thanks for coming to get me."

Moments later, back-up arrived and an ambulance was called for Nick just to check him over. Once Farrell and Fairbanks had been taken away to the station, the two detectives got back in the car and prepared to head to the hospital so they could explain everything to Nick's parents. "I think I'm more nervous about this than I was going into that house," Saunders said drily.

Sealey smiled, "Yeah I know, I'm dreading it too. But look, the important thing is we got Nick back. We'll just have to accept whatever his parents or the boss throws at us I suppose."

Saunders nodded and looked Sealey in the eye, "Listen, you did a great job today. I never thought I'd say this but we make a good team. Thanks Karen."

"Karen!" Sealey gawped in surprise, "Well I am honoured. We do make a good team though. Thanks Mike."

"Hey, I never said you can use my first name." Saunders smiled as he pulled the car away and headed for the hospital.

Chapter thirty

Sealey and Saunders wearily sat themselves down in a booth in the corner of the pub just around the corner from the police station. It had been a long day and they were both tired but they felt they should celebrate their victory. "Well, all things considered, I think we can call this whole case a success!" said Sealey with a fair share of sarcasm in her voice. "Cheers!"

"Cheers." Saunders tapped his drink against Sealey's glass and began to drink his pint; it tasted great. "My ears are still ringing after the abuse Mrs. Knight threw at us."

"I know," nodded Sealey, "thank God Nick and his dad calmed her down in the end. I think it's safe to say that Nick inherits his calmness from his father. To be fair though, she was well within her rights to go off like that. If someone had screwed up like we did with one of my kids, I'd go mental too."

"Do you think she'll make a complaint?" asked Saunders.

Sealey thought for a bit while she sipped her glass of white wine. "No, I don't think Nick would ever forgive her if she did."

"Let's hope you're right. If he does stop her, that'll be the second thing I owe him for. He's a good kid. I think I'm gonna miss him in a weird way." Saunders admitted. Sealey nearly choked on her drink. "That'll be the drink talking! Anyway, you'll see him again at the trial. What about the boss? What do you think he's gonna say about all this?"

"Well, I've already spoken to Terry and he's agreed to keep his mouth shut about it all. No surprise really, seeing as he was the one who let Fairbanks snatch Nick. The only other person who knows about it is Malcolm and he's already made it clear he wants to be totally disassociated with the whole thing. So, as long as Mrs. Knight stays quiet," Saunders explained, crossing his fingers, "we might just get away with it!"

"I'll drink to that." Sealey said, holding her glass in the air.

"No, let's drink to Nick, he's a brave kid. To Nick."

"To Nick" Sealey and Saunders tapped their glasses again and drank the rest of their drinks in silence.

Nick was discharged from hospital very quickly. The doctor said he was fine and the bruising around his wrists from being tied to the chair would subside normally. Nick thought he would have to call the doctor back to check his hearing after his mum launched a torrent of abuse at Saunders and Sealey over what had happened. He couldn't be mad or embarrassed by her; after all he thought he'd never see her again a few hours ago. Eventually he and his dad managed to calm her down and the Knight family went home. Nick slept very heavily and didn't wake up until 11.30 the next morning.

Over the next few days, Nick's mum wouldn't let him go to school, insisting he needed to recover from his ordeal. He thought this was great at first but her constant fussing started to drive him mad so Nick ended up saying he wanted to go back to school!

When he returned to school, he received a hero's welcome from Martin and his friends. Martin, as usual, had been unable to keep quiet about what had happened and everyone was desperate to find out what had happened to Nick. He showed them his bruises, which had almost faded, and told them about the knife (although he missed out the part where he cried). Eventually though, everything went back to normal.

Seven weeks after the day of his kidnap, Nick had to go to court for the trial of Leon Fairbanks and Charlie Farrell. It was great to see Saunders and Sealey again, even his mum smiled at them begrudgingly. Surprisingly, Nick was not at all nervous about the trial; he knew this was the last thing he had to do before this whole ordeal ended. Nick did exactly as he had been told; he spoke clearly and kept to the facts about what had happened. When he explained about Farrell producing the knife, he saw some of the women in the jury shaking their heads sadly. There was some talk from the Panther members' lawyer about warrants which Nick did not really understand but the police seemed to explain that argument away. After the trial, Nick, Saunders and Sealey went for a McDonalds while they waited for the jury to decide their verdict. The detectives were quiet and Nick could sense their nervousness about what the decision would be. The jury took three hours for deliberation and as the Head Juror stood to announce their verdict, Nick too felt very uneasy. Thankfully, both Farrell and Fairbanks were found guilty – Farrell was sentenced to 4 years in prison while Fairbanks, who was on a higher charge, got 9 years.

As Nick left the courthouse with Saunders and Sealey and his family behind them, a crowd of photographers and reporters shouted questions at them. Nick didn't really listen to them, he just thought 'so this is what it's like to be famous' and let the police and the lawyers answer the questions. The next day, Nick's ordeal made the front page of local and national newspapers. His dad bought copies of each one. Nick's favourite had the headline:

HERO, 11, PUTS GANG LEADER AND KILLER IN JAIL
NICK THE KNIGHT IN SHINING ARMOUR

Despite the awful gag on his name, he liked the fact he was called a hero so he cut it out, laminated it, put it in a frame and hung it on his wall. The coolest thing was the warrant card that Saunders and Sealey had made for him. "Every police officer has one of these, Nick" Saunders explained.
"We were so impressed by you that we thought you deserved one." Sealey added.
Nick shook their hands and said, "Thanks, I'll keep it until I get my real one when I'm older."

THE END

Printed in Great Britain
by Amazon.co.uk, Ltd.,
Marston Gate.